Mrs Rainbow

A

BOOK

Published by STORYSACK LTD
Resource House   Kay Street
BURY BL9 6BU

ISBN 0-9537099-1-4

Copyright Neil Griffiths 2000

First published in the UK 2000

Printed in the UK
by Carlton Press Group
Units 4 to 7 Britannia Road
Sale, Cheshire
M33 2AA

Mrs Rainbow

a colourful story
written by
Neil Griffiths
and illustrated by
Judith Blake

STORYSACK LTD

This book was inspired by

Jenny Rainbow

and is dedicated to the memory of my Mum,

a lovely lady who brought a rainbow into many people's lives.

Mrs Rainbow

This is the house where Mrs Rainbow lives: just
wait until you see what it's like inside!

She has painted the kitchen bright green, the conservatory a warm orange and the sitting room soothing shades of yellow.

Upstairs the bathroom is ocean blue, the study a welcoming red and the guest room a restful violet.

Mrs Rainbow's own bedroom however, is decorated in one of her favourite colours, indigo, and there you will find every shade of purple imaginable!

Mrs Rainbow is never happier than when relaxing
in her garden. Here she is now, sitting in her
favourite spot enjoying a glass of cool lemonade.

She loves her garden at all times of the year

with the reds, golds and browns of autumn,

the silvers and whites of winter

and the yellows, purples and greens of spring...

... but summer is Mrs Rainbow's favourite season and today her garden looks at its best.

However, Mrs Rainbow can't relax for too long today as the Village School is holding a car-boot sale and she is keen to get there early to pick up some bargains.

She is the first to arrive and can hardly wait to get started. Nothing excites Mrs Rainbow more than the thought of finding something unexpected to add to her colourful home.

After an hour's hunting, she emerges smiling from the school playground clutching a bright orange candle for the conservatory, a burgundy patchwork cushion for the study, a purple mug for her night-time hot chocolate drink and a turquoise soap dish - she will have to decide later whether this will be for the bathroom or the kitchen.

On her way home, the sky began to cloud over
and light drizzle fell.

By the time she reached the house, it had turned
into a very grey day indeed and Mrs Rainbow was
glad to get inside.

On days like this, Mrs Rainbow usually kept busy,
working on her latest painting or putting the
finishing touches to a tapestry. Sometimes she
just sat and watched her tropical fish, dazzled by
their stunning colours.

Today was different. Mrs Rainbow had hardly got
her coat off before she had rushed upstairs to try
out the new hair colour she had bought at the
chemist.

The bottle said "Bermuda Blonde" but, as she emerged from the wash basin, blonde it certainly was not; more a "Peacock Green"!

"Perfect!" thought Mrs Rainbow as she admired herself in the bathroom mirror.

She had barely finished drying her hair when there was a loud knock at the front door.

She was greeted by three somewhat startled
members of the District Council Planning Department
(shocked perhaps by the colour of Mrs Rainbow's
hair or by her matching outfit!).

"G - g - good afternoon, madam", stuttered a stout
gentleman wearing a black pin-stripe suit and a
bowler hat.

They explained that they were from the Planning
Department and handed a letter to Mrs Rainbow to
read.

Blackford

The District Council
Planning Office
Greyfriars Road
BLACKFORD
Co. Dullham

To the occupant of "Rainbow Cottage"

At our recent monthly planning meeting, it was decided that your house "Rainbow Cottage" was not in keeping with the rest of the village.

*It was agreed that the cottage was far too colourful and must immediately be painted **grey** to match all the other buildings.*

*Signed: The District Council
                Planning Committee*

Mrs Rainbow tried to protest, as she loved her little cottage and thought everybody else did.

But the councillors would not change their decision and said they were sorry but rules were rules and the painters would start work promptly in the morning.

As they left, Mrs Rainbow looked sadly at the houses in the village beyond before removing her house sign and gently closing the door behind her.

As promised, the painters arrived promptly the following morning and quickly set to work. They too felt sad but were only following the Council's orders.

Mrs Rainbow was nowhere to be seen and the curtains to the cottage remained strangely drawn all day.

News quickly spread to the other villagers through
Mrs Braithwaite, who had almost ridden her
bicycle off the road and through the hedge when
she caught sight of the newly painted cottage.

Soon a large, inquisitive crowd had gathered
outside, hardly able to believe its eyes.

It was the Reverend Fowler who finally plucked up
enough courage to knock on the door and ask
Mrs Rainbow how she was feeling.

After some time she appeared looking pale and grey. She thanked the villagers for their concern and said that she was feeling a little off colour today, before returning into the darkness of the cottage.

The worried villagers hurried to the Village Hall
where a special meeting was called to discuss the
situation.

Several hours later, they emerged looking very
pleased with themselves.

Early the next morning, even before the sun had risen, a long queue had formed outside Fred Stanley's DIY Store. It seemed as if the whole village were there.

The following day, the Reverend Fowler, accompanied by a large, excited crowd, gathered outside Mrs Rainbow's cottage. He knocked on the door and asked her to step out into the front garden since they had a surprise for her which would bring the colour back into her life.

Mrs Rainbow, still looking pale and grey, shuffled nervously out of the doorway and stood in silent amazement. She could hardly believe her eyes.

The Reverend Fowler had painted the Vicarage
purple and plum, whilst the Post Office was a
startling scarlet! Jean's Hair Salon was now pastel
shades of lilac and peach, the "Crossroads Cafe"

a rich maroon and the Library emerald green. In
fact, every house and building in the village had
been newly painted in the most glorious colours -
even the Church had a bright new yellow steeple!

Tears streamed down Mrs Rainbow's face. She had
never seen anything so beautiful.

"You did this all for me?" she asked.

The villagers nodded and smiled proudly.

Mrs Rainbow sat staring at the patchwork of colour
until darkness fell and, as she reluctantly made her
way indoors, the moonlight caught the top of the
church steeple and it shone like a golden star over
the village. Mrs Rainbow felt very happy indeed.

Several days later, the District Councillors returned to the cottage with another important letter for Mrs Rainbow to read:

The District Council
Planning Office
Greyfriars Road
BLACKFORD
Co. Dullham

To Mrs Rainbow

At our recent monthly planning meeting, it was decided unanimously that your house "un-named" was not in keeping with the rest of the village. It was agreed that your cottage is far too dull and should be painted in the brightest of colours immediately.

Signed:

The District Council
Planning Committee

Mrs Rainbow could hardly contain her excitement and hugged each of the councillors (much to their embarrassment) before rushing into the village to tell everyone the wonderful news.

After a visit to Fred Stanley's DIY Store, she invited the whole village to a 'Painting Party' to thank them for their kindness.

The cottage was soon restored to its original beauty
and that afternoon the villagers enjoyed a delicious
and colourful afternoon tea.

The party was briefly interrupted by a sudden
change in the weather as a summer shower forced
everyone to rush inside. However, on their return
to the garden they were treated to a beautiful
surprise.

As Mrs Rainbow admired the colourful scene, she noticed that it wasn't only the weather that was changing!

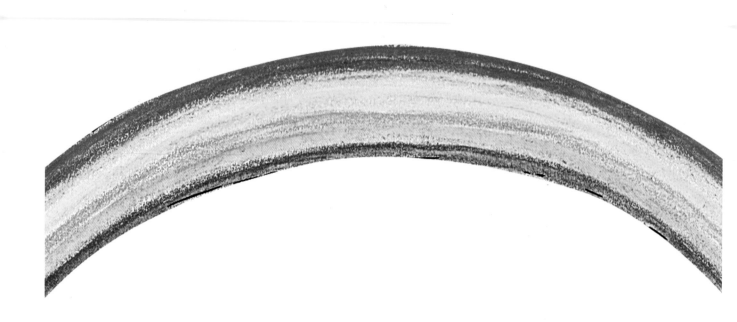

The end.

Other titles by Storysack

If Only (also available in Welsh)
ISBN 0-9540498-4-5

Teddy takes a tumble
ISBN 0 9540498 8 8

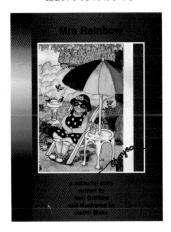

Mrs Rainbow
ISBN 0-9537099-1-4

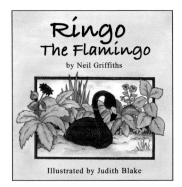

Ringo The Flamingo
ISBN 0-9540498-2-9

Grandma Brown
ISBN 0-9537099-7-3

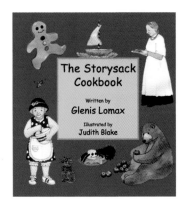

The Storysack Cookbook
ISBN 0-9540498-7X

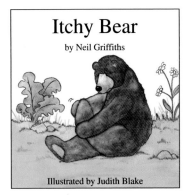

Itchy Bear
ISBN 0-9540498-10
Also available in big book form

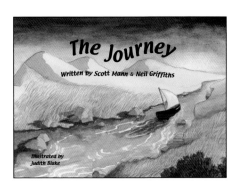

The Journey
ISBN 0-9540498-0-2
Also available in big book form

www.storysack.com